To Wisteria,
the girl who roars

A FEIWEL AND FRIENDS BOOK
An Imprint of Macmillan

Feiwel and Friends books may be purchased for business or promotional use.
For information on bulk purchases, please contact the Macmillan Corporate and Premium Sales Department
at (800) 221-7945 x5442 or by e-mail at specialmarkets@macmillan.com.

Library of Congress Cataloging-in-Publication Data Available

ISBN: 978-1-250-01689-8

Feiwel and Friends logo designed by Filomena Tuosto
The artwork was created with oils on paper.

First Edition: 2014

1 3 5 7 9 10 8 6 4 2

mackids.com

OH SO BRAVE DRAGON

story and paintings by

DAVID KIRK

Feiwel and Friends
New York

I may be little,
but I am brave.
Oh so brave!

See my bravery
as I flap my oh so mighty wings!
As I blast my oh so fearsome breath.
I fear nothing!

Hear my courage
as I bellow my first
oh so valiant . . .

What was that noise?

Was that me?

No, that wasn't me.

That couldn't have been

MY roar....

I'm pretty sure.

What terrifying beast could have made
that awful noise—a Mountain Shark?
an Ow Bird? a Grizzle Bear?
I will frighten it away!

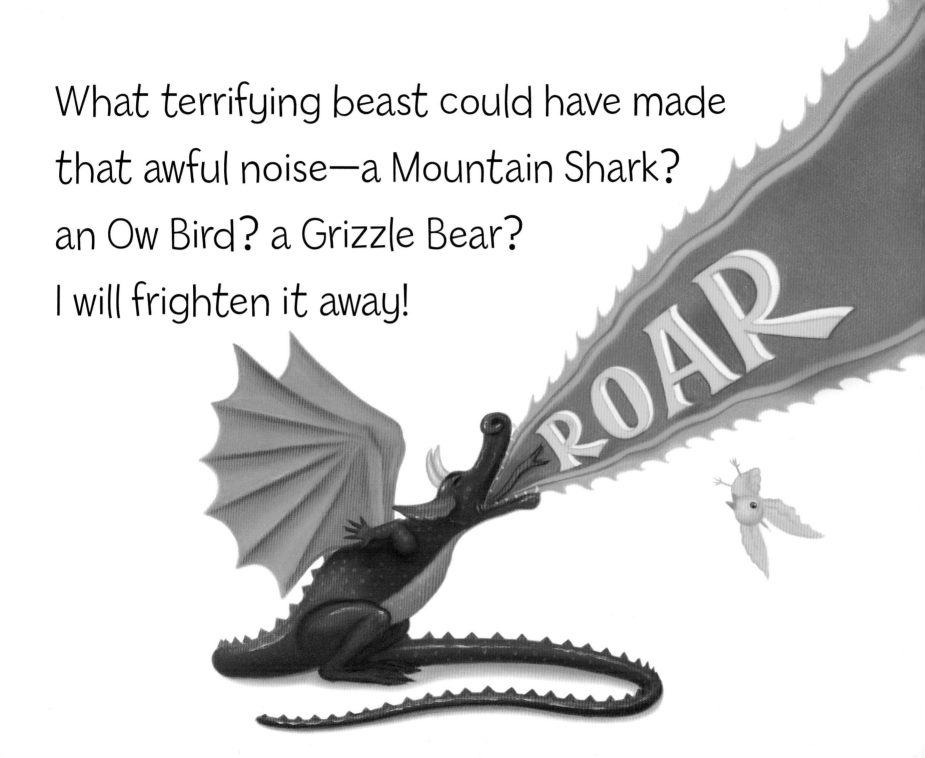

I heard it again! Yes, I know I roared, but there was something else. Didn't you hear it?

Just listen. Something is lurking!

Did you hear the monster?

Did *you* hear the monster?

Did *you* hear the monster?

Did *you* hear the monster?

Did *you* hear the monster?

Did you *all* hear the monster?

The monster is near!

I'll protect you. Come in close.

We'll roar together and scare it away!

ROAR!

Again
ROAR!
Again
ROAR!
Again
ROAR!

I'm sure the monster is gone now,
but let's all stay here just in case,
where we can be oh so brave . . .

together.